D0607946

DR. DRABBLE, GENIUS INVENTOR

Dr. Drabble's Remarkable Underwater Breathing Pills
Dr. Drabble's Spectacular Shrinker-Enlarger
Dr. Drabble and the Dynamic Duplicator

Copyright © 1994 by Word Publishing
All rights reserved. No portion of this book may be reproduced in any
form without the written permission of the publisher, except for brief
excerpts in reviews.

(Revised version of an earlier publication. Originally published as
Dr. Drabble's Incredible Identical Robot Innovation
© 1992 by SP Publications, Inc.)

ISBN: 0-8499-3660-8

Printed in the United States of America
94 95 96 97 98 99 LBM 9 8 7 6 5 4 3 2 1

Dr. Drabble

and the
Dynamic Duplicator

DR. DRABBLE
AND THE
DYNAMIC DUPLICATOR

Written by
Sigmund Brouwer and Wayne Davidson
Illustrated by
Bill Bell

WORD PUBLISHING
Dallas·London·Vancouver·Melbourne

*With love,
to Kerri Lynn*

P. J. and Chelsea flew on Dr. Drabble's Flying Ship to a tropical island in the South Pacific.

On the island, P. J. and his pet skunk Wesley played with a friendly monkey. The monkey hung upside down from a tree. P. J. also hung upside down.

The monkey let go and jumped down. P. J. was afraid to let go and jump down.

P. J.'s sister, Chelsea, decided to help him down by tickling him under the arm.

"Aaaaagh!" P. J. screamed. He fell exactly six inches.

Just then, they heard Dr. Drabble yell, "P. J., Chelsea, HELP!"

The kids ran into the laboratory and saw Dr. Drabble trying to carry a huge stack of coconuts. Suddenly, Dr. Drabble tripped and coconuts flew everywhere.

"Coconuts!" Chelsea giggled. "Why do you need coconuts?"

"For my new invention." Dr. Drabble pointed at a strange and wonderful machine. "It uses coconuts for fuel."

"What does the machine do?" P. J. asked.

"I'll show you, but you must promise never to use the machine when I'm not here," said Dr. Drabble.

"Arnie, would you please step inside the machine?" asked Dr. Drabble. Arnie Clodbuckle was Dr. Drabble's assistant.

Arnie stepped inside and Dr. Drabble put a few coconuts in the top of the machine. He pulled a switch. The machine rumbled. Smoke filled the air. Then there was silence. Arnie stepped out.

"What's so great about that?" Chelsea asked.

Another Arnie stepped out.

"This is the Dynamic Duplicator," Dr. Drabble explained. "It comes out with one Arnie and one duplicate."

"I don't want a duplicate," moaned Arnie.

"Then throw water on it," Dr. Drabble said. "The duplicate will turn into bubbles and float away."

P. J. and Chelsea went with Arnie to get more coconuts. When they reached the trees, Arnie realized that he had forgotten the ladder.

Suddenly a monkey chattered from behind them.

Chelsea saw their monkey friend had an idea.

"I'll give him my red scarf and ask him to throw the coconuts to us."

Soon the monkey began to throw down buckets and buckets of coconuts.

Arnie forgot to duck. Coconuts bounced off his head.

"Ouch!" he cried. "I'm going back to the ship!"

The monkey helped P. J. and Chelsea carry coconuts back to Dr. Drabble's Flying Ship.

"This is too much work. Let's create a duplicate monkey to help us carry the rest of the coconuts," said Chelsea.

Before P. J. could say anything, Chelsea was throwing coconuts in the machine. "Stop Chelsea," P. J. yelled, as he tried to grab a coconut from the machine. "We promised Dr. Drabble we wouldn't . . ."

But it was too late. Chelsea had filled the machine with coconuts, put the monkey inside, and shut the door. Quickly, Chelsea pulled the lever.

The Dynamic Duplicator shook and rumbled and smoked.

"Push the lever back!" P. J. shouted above the noise.

"I can't!" Chelsea shouted back. "It's stuck!"

The machine finally stopped and P. J. opened the door. Their monkey friend hopped out and grinned.

Chelsea opened the other door. Another monkey jumped out.

"See," Chelsea said. "Nothing went wrong."

A third monkey hopped out. Then a fourth. Soon the room was filled with monkeys.

They chattered and they screeched. They swung from the ceiling, and grabbed books from the shelves. They pulled at levers, and they pushed at buttons. They even ate Arnie's secret chocolate chip cookie collection.

Dr. Drabble, Arnie, and Wesley heard the noise and hurried into the laboratory.

Dr. Drabble ran to the fire hose and sprayed water. All but one of the monkeys became bubbles and slowly floated out the window. The one monkey left was wet and grumpy. He jumped out the window and ran away.

"You used the Dynamic Duplicator after you promised you wouldn't," Dr. Drabble said sadly.

"We're very sorry," P. J. and Chelsea said together.

"Okay, I accept your apology," Dr. Drabble told them. "Now clean this mess up and promise me you won't ever use it again, all right?"

"Yes, sir," they both said.

Dr. Drabble left with Arnie.

P. J. grumbled, "This was all your idea." He kicked at a coconut.

"I have a better idea," Chelsea grinned. "We can make duplicates of ourselves and make THEM clean the laboratory. Then we can find our monkey friend and play."

P. J. frowned. "But we just promised that we wouldn't use the Dynamic Duplicator again."

"Maybe Dr. Drabble meant not to use the machine to make more monkeys," Chelsea offered. "Besides, we'll only use a few coconuts, and we'll be really careful."

P. J. finally agreed. He wanted to go outside and play, too.

P. J. and Chelsea found their monkey friend and apologized. They played for hours while the children's duplicates cleaned the laboratory.

Then Chelsea started feeling bad about breaking her promise.

P. J. felt the same way.

At supper, their mom said, "You both look upset. Aren't you happy about the double allowance we gave you for cleaning up the laboratory?"

"Double allowance?" Chelsea repeated.

"Don't you remember?" Mom said. "I gave it to you this afternoon, along with your presents."

"Presents?" P. J. squeaked.

Chelsea's face turned pale. P. J. gulped.

"We didn't get any presents," Chelsea said quietly.

"But we gave them to you," Mom insisted.

"I wish that were true," Chelsea said. "But we made duplicates of ourselves this afternoon in Dr. Drabble's new machine. They cleaned the laboratory, and we went out to play. You must have given the gifts and allowance to them."

"I suppose that serves us right," P. J. added. "We broke our promise to Dr. Drabble."

Then Mom and Dad took P. J. and Chelsea out on the ship's deck for a talk.

Chelsea said, "I'm really sorry. I will apologize to Dr. Drabble, too."

"Yeah," said P. J. "We know we were wrong to break our promise."

"But we're glad that you confessed," Mom said.

Dad put his arms around Chelsea and P. J. "Because we see that you are very sorry, your mom and I forgive you."

"I bet those presents are still somewhere on the ship. We will help you look for them," Mom added.

"Thanks!" said Chelsea. "You are so nice, I wish I could make two more of you in Dr. Drabble's Dynamic Duplicator!"

"Chelsea!" Dad warned.

"Chelsea!" Mom giggled.

Chelsea smiled. "Just kidding."